Vera B. Williams

Lucky Song

Greenwillow Books New York

Watercolor paints were used for the full-color art. The text type is Gorilla. Copyright © 1997 by Vera B. Williams.
All rights reserved. No part of this book may be reproduced. Published by Greenwillow Books,
a division of William Morrow & Company, Inc., 1350 Avenue of the Americas, New York, NY 10019.
Printed in Singapore by Tien Wah Press. First Edition 10 9 8 7 6 5 4 3 2 1
Library of Congress Cataloging-in-Publication Data: Williams, Vera B. Lucky song / by Vera B. Williams.
p. cm. ISBN 0-688-14459-4 (trade). ISBN 0-688-14460-8 (lib. bdg.)
[1. Day—Fiction. 2. Kites—Fiction. 3. Singing—Fiction.]
I. Title. PZ7.W6685Lu 1997 [E]—dc20 96-7151 CIP AC

Now this little Evie wanted to do something,

so she got ready.

She wanted something new to wear,

and on the hook she found it.

She wanted something new to play with,

and her grandpa made it for her.

She wanted to go out,

and the door flew open.

She wanted to run up a steep hill,

and her legs carried her.

She wanted to fly her kite.

and the wind took it.

When she shouted, "Look how high!"

her mother   ran to look.

When she wanted to go home for supper,

her grandma had it ready.

When she wanted her blanket,

her sister wrapped it around her.

When she wanted a song,

her father came and sang to her—

all about Evie, who flew her kite

up with the clouds and the speedy planes.

If you want to hear that song again,
go back to the beginning.